Louie's Search

EZRA JACK KEATS

PUFFIN BOOKS

PUFFIN BOOKS
Published by the Penguin Group
Penguin Putnam Books for Young Readers, 345 Hudson Street, New York, New York 10014, U.S.A.
Penguin Books Ltd, 27 Wrights Lane, London W8 5TZ, England
Penguin Books Australia Ltd, Ringwood, Victoria, Australia
Penguin Books Canada Ltd, 10 Alcorn Avenue, Toronto, Ontario, Canada M4V 3B2
Penguin Books (N.Z.) Ltd, 182-190 Wairau Road, Auckland 10, New Zealand

Penguin Books Ltd, Registered Offices: Harmondsworth, Middlesex, England

First published in the United States of America by Four Winds Press, 1980
Published by Viking and Puffin Books, divisions of Penguin Putnam Books for Young Readers, 2001

10 9 8 7

Library of Congress Cataloging-in-Publication Data
Keats, Ezra Jack. Louie's search / Ezra Jack Keats.   p.   cm.
Summary: After moving to a busy new neighborhood with his mother, Louie
decides to explore and see if there is anyone he might like to have as a father.
ISBN 0-670-89224-6 (hardcover) — ISBN 0-14-056761-5 (pbk.)
[1. City and town life—Fiction. 2. Fathers—Fiction. 3. Remarriage—Fiction.]
I. Title.   PZ7.K2253 Lr 2001   [E]—dc21   00-009594

Puffin Books ISBN 978-0-14-056761-8

Manufactured in China

To Dean Engel

"What kind of neighborhood is this?"
thought Louie.

"Nobody notices a kid around here."
Louie put on some funny things and
took a walk.

Maybe someone would notice him—
someone he'd like for a father.

Louie passed quite a few people.
He looked them over,
and walked on.

People were going up and down,
and in and out.
He wanted to say something to them,
but they were too busy.

Louie walked backward,
still looking at them.
He bumped into a man
carrying a big cake.

"Watch where you're going!"
the man yelled.
Louie turned around
and walked forward.

He saw a truck piled high with old furniture.

As he got closer, something fell off.

Louie picked it up to put it back.

It began to play music!

The man in the truck turned around.

He looked terrible!

"Hey!" he yelled. "What are you doing with that?"

Louie was so scared, he couldn't speak.

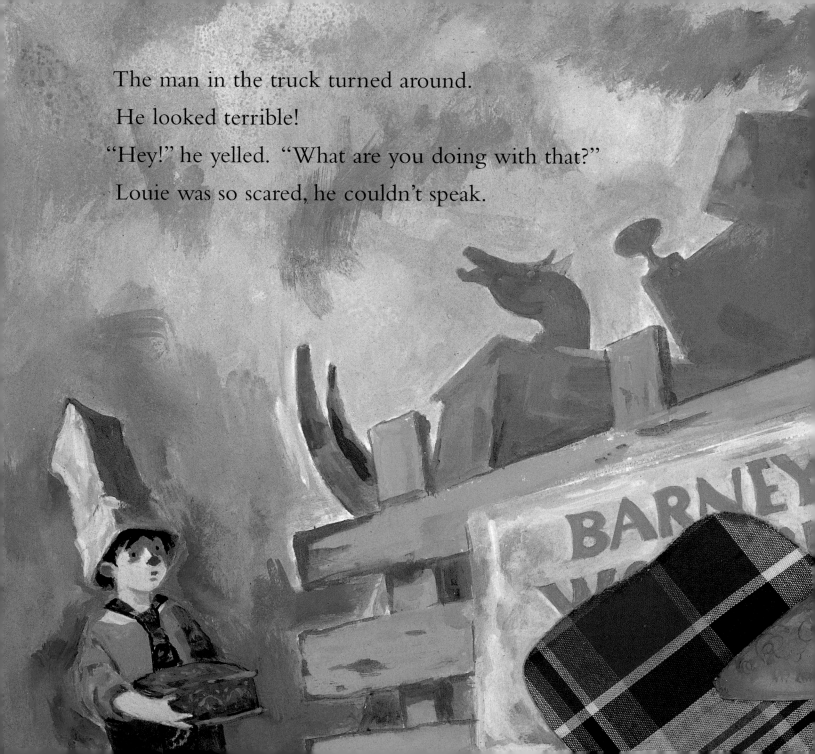

BARNEY

The man jumped off the truck, and chased Louie.
"Come back, you little crook!" he bellowed.

Louie fell!

The man stared down at him.

"You stole it!" he shouted. "Where do you live?"

"No, I didn't steal it," Louie cried. "Ow! Ow! My foot!"

Louie pointed to where he lived.

They went into his house.

"Louie! What happened?" his mother gasped. "And who are you?"

"Your son's a crook!"

"What? IMPOSSIBLE! He's the best boy in the world!"

"Ow! Ow! He broke my foot!" Louie cried.

"Really? You're still standing on it—and what's that music I hear?"

Louie saw that he was still holding the box.

He dropped it.

BANG! It stopped playing.

"Now you broke my beautiful music maker!" the man boomed.
"You'll pay for this!"

The house got quiet.

"WELL, WHAT ARE YOU GOING TO DO?"

the man shouted, shaking his fists in the air.

The whole room shook. The music box began to play.

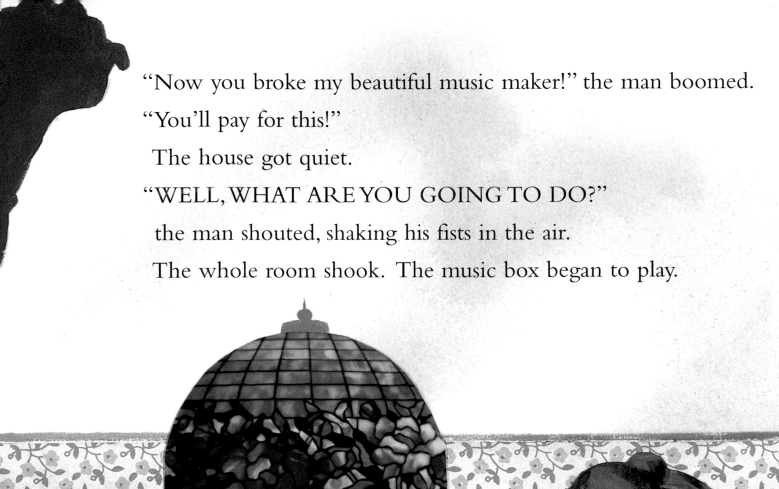

The man looked around, surprised.
"Err—ya know what? That thing never
played like that for me before,"
said the man.

"See? And you blamed Louie," his mother said.

"If I know him, he was only trying to put it back."

Louie nodded.

"Well—in that case—I'm sorry," the man mumbled.

He picked up the box and started to leave.

Then he turned around and said,

"Since it plays so good for you, Louie,

why don't you keep it? Here's the windup key."

Louie jumped up and down.

His foot felt fine.

"By the way," said the man, "my name's Barney,"
and he bowed a little.

"My name's Peg, and, of course, you know my son, Louie."

"Hello," said Louie. "Do you have a boy of your own?"

"Nope. Just me and my business."

"Would you like a cup of tea?" asked Peg.

A few days later Barney returned.

He took them in his truck to the waterfront.

Barney knew just about everybody!

The tugboat men gave them a ride on their boat.

Barney visited Louie and Peg again and again.

Then, one Sunday, at the end of summer . . .

Barney and Peg got married!
They had a wonderful wedding.
And all their friends and neighbors came.